Grace and Scout

by Michele Morgan & Lauren Lovejoy

ISBN-10: 1976292727

ISBN-13: 978-1976292729

The text of this book is set in Calisto 13 pt font.

The illustrations in this book were created digitally.

Written for the nonprofit, Lyme Warrior

LYME WARRIOR

http://lymewarrior.us/

Two fast friends, Grace and Scout,

Made mischief and mayhem as they played about.

They built forts and sand castles and played in the snow,

But on one Spring day that wouldn't be so.

This is the story of Grace and Scout,

And what being a true friend is all about.

On one cool day in the month of May, Scout couldn't find Grace.
She wasn't in class or outside to play.

Scout came home and asked his Mom, "Mom, where is Grace? Is she away?"

His Mom said, "Sit down Little Scout, I need you to be brave.

Grace is ill and having some tough days."

She continued and told him that Grace was sick.
All from the bite of a tiny little tick.

Scout looked confused. "How can that be? I played with her!
Will it happen to me?"

Scouts Mom reassured him, "This is why I check your hair.
Mist you with bug spray, and make sure that your legs aren't bare.'

"But ticks are quite small and are curious things,
And sometimes it happens that we don't see a thing."

HIKING TRAIL

SCOUT'S
HOME

Scout felt sad and a bit angry too.

He hoped Grace would be well real soon.

Scout asked his mom, "Will she ever come out?"
His Mom said, "Yes, but Grace needs hope and a friend,
And that friend is YOU Scout."

Scout yelled, "You're right Mom!" and ran up to his room.

He pulled out his paper, glitter, crayons and glue.

He worked hard on this project. It was special you see.

"Grace needs a friend and that friend is me!"

When he was done, Scout admired his card.

He thought to himself. This is awesome!! My very best work of art!

He yelled down to his Mom, "Can we go see Grace?
I have something special and it cannot wait!"

Scout ran to Grace's house, which was right down the street.
He was excited and nervous and not sure what to think.

Grace's Mom quietly answered the ding.

Seeing Scout's excitement was a wonderful thing.

She hugged him and gently said, "Grace is resting on the couch.

But first let me tell you something sweet little Scout.

Grace is quite sick and incredibly weak, but she could sure use a smile and it is your friendship she needs."

Scout was happy and a little scared too, but he walked down the hall and into the room.

Grace's face lit up when she saw Scout walk in.

Scout puzzled and thought she doesn't look super sick.

But inside her, her heart had been made sick by that tick.

Scout eagerly asked "Grace are you ok?"
Grace said "I'm better, but still cannot play."

Scout reached into his backpack and pulled out the card,
The one he created and worked on so hard.

Grace's eyes grew big when she saw the sparkling colorful art.

Scout had cut the paper into a beautiful heart.

She opened the card and inside it read:

You're my very best friend. I'm sorry you're sick!

Love,

Get wEll
soon.
P.S. I'm mad
at that
tick!

Scout

Months went by and every day
Scout looked for Grace at school,
But she was still away.

As Scout laid down every night he would say,

"I hope you get well Grace, and can't wait to play."

After such a long time. It felt like forever.

Grace seemed to be feeling a little bit better.

Scout saw her walk in as he sat at his desk,

He could tell right away she wasn't feeling her best.

He remembered his Mom's words about being brave.
And he marched up to Grace with a smile on his face.

He threw his arms around her neck and hugged her.
"Grace, tick bite or not, we are best friends forever."

This was the story of Grace and Scout.

I hope you've learned what being a true friend is about.

Friends have ups and friends have downs.

But a loving friend is always around.

Show kindness to friends, in your unique way.
So go and be brave. Don't let fear guide your days.

Dear Parents,

Tick Borne illnesses can be problematic for children that are active and who love the outdoors. For parents, the best way to stop tick borne illness is to prevent it from happening. Here are some great prevention tips for you and your children.

1. Wearing light colored clothing is the best way to visualize ticks if they have gotten onto your clothes. Tuck long pants into socks for added protection in the fall and early spring!

2. Washing with a natural insect repellent soap bar prior to going outdoors is highly recommended. Such soap likely contains one or more of the following ingredients: rosemary, garlic, lemon grass, Neem, eucalyptus, or geranium.

3. You can make your own natural tick repellent that is safe for your children and your pets. Use 20 drops lemon grass essential oil; 20 drops eucalyptus essential oil; 4oz water; add to a clean spray bottle, and shake well. We recommend using this repellent every 1-2 hours.

4. Be sure to perform a head-to-toe check of your children when they come in from outdoors. Nymph ticks can be as small as poppy seeds. Removing ticks should be done with a specific tool, and if saved, it is important to send your ticks out to be tested. More information on this at www.tickreport.com.

5. For parents, "Tick tubes" can be a great asset to your backyard. These are 2" diameter PVC that are filled with cotton balls, that are then are immersed in permethrin insect repellent, that can be placed around the peripheral of your backyard, every 20 feet. They will attract mice which will go into the tube, and the ticks will be killed off of the mice, while the mouse itself will remain unharmed.

6. Guinea hens eat up to 5,000 ticks per week. If you live in a rural area, parents can invest in and care for this animal - it is a great way to "clean up" your yard from those pesky ticks.

Be safe, be protected and be well!

Dr. Ronald L. Stram
Stram Center for Integrative Medicine
www.stramcenter.com

Made in the USA
Lexington, KY
24 March 2018